I0692242

THE UNFORGETTABLE ADVENTURE

by
Sophia Zhong

Illustrations by
Brad Appleby

Published by

The Unforgettable Adventure

Published in the United States of America
by Goddaughtersink.com
Available from Amazon.com
www.sophiazhong.com
and other retail outlets.

Dedications

This book is dedicated to my family, including my godparents, who have always encouraged me to follow my interests. Thank you for being with me. I'm lucky to have you in my life.

- Sophia Zhong

Illustrations in this book are dedicated to DeAnne and Sophia, who both love making changes to my illustrations even before I start. It is only because of their constant judgement and endless criticism that my art gets better. Thank you both. It's a good thing!

- Brad Appleby

THE UNFORGETTABLE ADVENTURE

"Wow! This is amazing! It's sooooo… beautiful!" Alicia Vanschink said breathlessly as she gazed at the forest around her. Alicia, a New Yorker, was used to the hectic chaos of the big city and found the Amazon Rainforest surprising and wonderful, an exciting, quiet place full of things to do and sights to see.

She turned to face her parents. "We're going to have a great adventure. It seems like anything can happen here. We may even see a ghost!" Her laughter rang through the trees. Little did she know just how accurate that prediction would turn out to be.

Alicia's father was a zookeeper, and his company had transferred him to the Amazon Zoo for the summer. The family was camping at Haunted Woods National Park in their RV until they could find a house to rent. Alicia had already claimed her spot in the RV: The bunk above the driver's seat.

Alicia had read all about the Amazon Rainforest, and she couldn't wait to see jaguars, sloths, scarlet macaws, and pink river dolphins. She was ready to explore.

"Alicia, you'd better rest up," her mother called. "We're going to be very busy tomorrow. Didn't you say you wanted to go sightseeing at the Amazon Museum?"

"Okay, Mom," Alicia called back. She climbed up into bed and lay there, thinking of the fun she would have the next day. She thought she would never fall asleep, but within ten minutes, she was out like a light.

The next morning, Alicia woke to a light rain shower. At first, she didn't want to get up, but then she remembered - the Amazon Museum! She clambered down from her bunk, checked the clock, and jumped onto her parents' bed.

"Wha…?" they muttered groggily, still half asleep.

"Come on! It's 8:00! The Amazon Museum opens at 9:00! I want to get there before the crowds. Let's go!" Alicia said excitedly. Her parents yawned, but they

obligingly got up, stretched, and began to get dressed while Alicia brushed her teeth.

The clock in the family's Jeep read 8:40 when they all finally hopped in. All the way to the museum, Alicia kept close track of the time. "Come on, come on, come on," she muttered through gritted teeth. She couldn't wait.

They made it…when the clock read 8:55. "Yes!" Alicia exclaimed as she jumped out of the Jeep. She ran to the ticket booth to make sure they were first in line. After her parents bought the tickets, they all walked into the museum. They were the first ones inside. The family went from exhibit to exhibit, and Alicia marveled at everything. She was especially interested in an exhibit called "The Mystery of Edgar Westcock." It had a plaque that read:

The Mystery of Edgar Westcock

Edgar Westcock was a man who lived in the 1930s. He owned a mansion in the Amazon Rainforest. He also had a zoo that he filled with Amazon animals: tapirs, poison dart frogs, pythons, and ocelots, to name a few. He managed to tame some of them, and they became his constant companions. Then, one night, he and all his pets disappeared. Vanished. Although people have searched, they have never found any trace of him or the missing animals. Even today, it is one of the strangest mysteries that has ever occurred in or around the Amazon.

Sophia Zhong

After Alicia and her parents explored the information part of the museum, she decided to visit the game section which taught people, especially kids, about the Amazon. Among other things, there was a rainforest simulation in the game section. By then her parents were tired, but they trusted Alicia so they let her go in by herself.

Halfway through the simulation, she stopped to look at some piranhas and read a plaque titled "Ferocious Fish." Then, suddenly, she experienced the strangest sensation. Her world went dark, and she felt as if she were falling.

When Alicia could see clearly again, she found herself in a beautiful sunlit clearing surrounded by a forest. Birds chirped happily in the trees around her. Through the leaves, Alicia saw the ruins of an old stone mansion,

Sophia Zhong

now covered with vines and ivy. She waited quietly, not knowing for what. She simply felt she had been brought here to do something.

After she had been standing there for a few minutes, she thought she saw something move in the trees. A strange voice said, "Do not be afraid of me." Something materialized out of the forest and solidified into a man.

The man wore the clothes of an explorer, and he hovered a few inches above the ground. He had brown eyes and hair, and he wore glasses. He would've been handsome, except for an arrow transfixing his head and stab marks on his chest.

Behind him, animals melted out of the shadows. A black panther with a studded collar, a monkey with a pink bow on its head, and a crocodile with a garland of colorful flowers around its neck, joined the mysterious man.

Alicia stared in shock and amazement as the man said, "I am Edgar Westcock, and I come with a warning. Heed it, and all will be well. Ignore it, and you shall regret it. Let me tell you the story of what happened to me. Listen to me, and listen carefully. This may save your father's life." Alicia instantly snapped to attention.

"That fateful night I disappeared, everything seemed normal at first. I went to bed, and most of my pets curled up in my bedroom with me, as usual. Around midnight, I was woken by a loud commotion. Jack," the panther flicked his ears, "was growling at the door that led to the hallway. Masie," the monkey nodded, "was riding Brunette," the crocodile stomped her foot, "and waving her special stick while Brunette snapped her jaws at the entrance. All my pets seemed very agitated. I blearily stumbled out of bed and opened the door to find out what was causing the ruckus. A young woman with a beautiful face, long, tumbling golden locks of hair and sky blue eyes was looking at me. The only thing that ruined the vision was those eyes. They blazed with fury. The last thing I remembered that night was her, raising a club and hitting me on the head."

"Who…who was this woman?" Alicia stammered, surprised. "Why would she want to hurt you?"

Edgar smiled sadly. "She was a member of the Amazon tribe. They had raided my home that night. They were angry because I was taking creatures from the rainforest, even though I was helping injured or orphaned animals. It wasn't my fault the animals wanted to stay with me or they couldn't survive in the wild, but the Amazons thought I should have let nature take its course." Edgar seemed lost in thought for a moment.

"Anyway, when I woke up," he continued, "I was in the Amazons' main camp, tied to a stake. In front of me was a huge tent. I looked around. To my right, I saw all of my pets in wooden enclosures. I was relieved they were all safe and well, though I did not yet know their fate…or mine. To my left, a young woman sat under a tree, sharpening arrows and watching me. I recognized her as the one who had hit me on the head. I studied her. Near her, she had a bow and a quiver of arrows, a sword, a club, and a hunting horn made out of bone. I was wondering where I was when something broke through my thoughts.

"'Dun-da-da-dun!' The sound of a horn echoed from the tent. The young woman shot

to her feet, pulled out her own horn, and blew. 'Da-da-da-dun!'

"A procession of females came out from the tent. A lovely young lady was leading it. She had intelligent dark eyes and shining, straight black hair that came to her shoulders. On her head was a leafy circlet of vines with flowers woven in. She wore a simple but elegant blue dress that swept the ground and gossamer ceremonial robes. She also had on a beautiful golden belt engraved with graceful designs. She seemed no older than eighteen, but I got the feeling she was much older than she appeared, because her dark eyes looked like they held much of the world's wisdom.

"She was confident, walked with a purposeful stride, and radiated an aura of power. Her youthful appearance made sense to me, since I knew that, as a blessing from

Ares and Artemis, Amazon royalty did not age unless they wished." Edgar paused, as if bracing himself for what was going to happen next.

"The young lady approached me while all the other women stood behind her in a half-circle. She looked straight at me and said, 'I am Queen Sapanaya of the Amazons. Tell us your story, and we will decide your fate.' So I told them everything."

"How did they take it?" Alicia asked.

"I was getting to that," Edgar replied. "After I finished telling them my story, the women went back into the tent for about an hour. When they came out again, they all looked solemn. Queen Sapanaya said, 'What you have done is unforgivable. You have taken the wild creatures of the gods from their natural homes and made them tame.

The punishment for this crime is death. I will allow you to choose the way you shall die: Water, fire, or weapon.' I chose weapon, as you can see.

"So my tale ends.

"I do not want this to happen to anyone else. My warning to you is this: The Amazons are unhappy because animals are once again being taken from the forest for the Amazon Zoo. Their fury has reached a boiling point. The Amazon Council has decided that Queen Sapanaya is going to personally lead a charge on the zoo - tonight."

"My father!" Alicia gasped. "He works at the zoo!"

"Alicia, our time together is over for now, but do not forget my warning. Beware."

Before she knew it he was gone, and Alicia was back in the museum alone, staring at the piranhas, her mind reeling at what she had just experienced: a ghost!

"Mom! Dad! You won't believe what I just saw!" Alicia yelled as she ran out of the rainforest simulation.

"Be quiet, be quiet!" her parents said, because she was getting some curious looks. After Alicia calmed down, she told them of her encounter. "It's just your imagination," they both said. "Forget it." They said it so many times she almost believed it. Soon after, the family left the museum and returned to the RV to rest.

The next day, Alicia begged to be taken back to the museum, even though her father was at work. Her mother consented. Alicia went to the rainforest simulation alone because her mother had to use the restroom. She nearly flew to the piranhas section, and when she arrived the same strange thing happened to her again. She was suddenly in the same clearing she had been in before, but now it was foggy and gloomy. Edgar and his pets soon appeared.

"I have some bad news. The Amazons raided the zoo last night and took some animals. They took the night watchman too," Edgar informed Alicia. Her eyes widened.

Edgar went on. "Alicia, you're the only living person who knows what's happening." Alicia knew what he was talking about. She also knew she would need proof to make anyone else even remotely believe her.

Alicia stretched up and picked a leaf from the nearest tree. "This might convince someone."

"Go," Edgar said. "Save your father and the zoo." Alicia nodded.

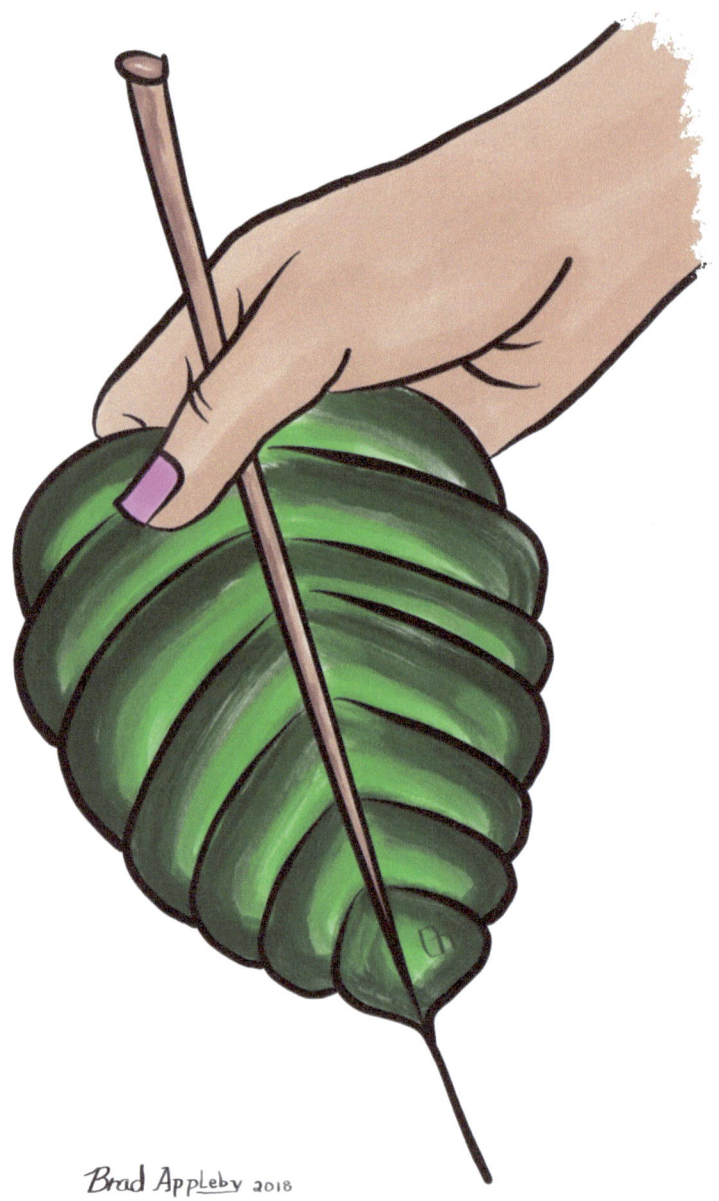

Brad Appleby 2018

Suddenly, she was in the rainforest simulation again. This time, she was one hundred and ten percent sure the meeting hadn't been a product of her imagination. Why? Because she held a large leaf tightly in her hand.

Alicia dashed out to meet her mother. "Mom! Dad is in danger!"

All of a sudden, she thought of another way to prove the zoo was being invaded. "Read the newspapers," she told her mom. "Someone raided the zoo last night and took some animals and the night watchman!"

Alicia ran outside to the nearest newsstand. "Which one has an article about the zoo raiding?" she asked the seller. The man pointed out the newspaper to her. She grabbed it, slammed some money down on the counter, and raced back inside the museum.

She found the piece and showed it to her mother. "Look, mom! Here's my proof that it really happened."

The article read:

Who Has Raided The Zoo?

On the evening of June 21st, something strange happened at the Amazon Zoo. The next morning, authorities found a large section of the fence knocked over and hoof prints on the ground around it. Residents living by the zoo reported hearing an unusual, chilling wolf howl, almost like a war-cry. Night watchman Ronald Donacker is gone, missing. The toucan, anaconda, and giant anteater enclosures are empty. No one knows what happened, although the police are working hard on the case. If you have any information about this raid on the zoo, please call the zoo hotline at 1-800-198-3605. Thank you.

- by Libby Reish

"See? I was right!" Alicia exclaimed.

"All right, so you knew about that. Do you have any other proof?" her mother asked.

"Yes, I do," Alicia said, showing her the leaf.

Her mother sighed. "You were in the rainforest simulation, Alicia. Of course you might have a leaf."

"No leaf in there looks like this. Come in with me and see for yourself," Alicia pressed.

"Fine," her mother said, going inside. Alicia showed her every single plant in the simulation.

"See, none of the leaves look like this one," Alicia said. "Now do you believe me?"

Her mother had one last question. "Why would Edgar tell you?"

"He knew I would believe him, and he knew someone I love works at the zoo. Mom, these attacks will keep going on until every zoo animal is freed. The Amazons will kill anyone who gets in their way. Dad has night duty tonight. We have to convince the zoo manager to take Dad off night watch. To do that, we have to call that number now and tell them what we know!"

"Fine, fine, fine. Go ahead and call," Alicia's mother relented. "But don't blame me if they refuse to meet with you or even

believe you," she warned, holding out her phone.

"Don't worry, I've got that all figured out. Thanks, Mom!" Alicia replied as she quickly dialed the number.

"This is the Amazon Zoo hotline. How may I help you?" a voice asked.

"Hi. Is this the number we call about the zoo raiding?" Alicia asked.

"Yes. Do you know something?" the voice asked.

"I know who raided the zoo. Can I arrange a meeting with the zoo manager?"

Half an hour later, Alicia was telling the zoo manager, whose name was Sharon Plarney, her story and showing her the leaf. Sharon's eyes widened when she saw the leaf.

"Where did you get that?" she demanded.

"I told you. In the clearing," Alicia said

impatiently. "Why do you look so surprised?"

"This is an aphandra leaf. It's very rare. It grows naturally only in the woods behind Edgar Westcock's mansion, and that's two hundred miles away from here," Sharon said in amazement as she carefully fingered the leaf. "Although I suppose that makes sense, considering what you're telling me," she added.

"If you don't believe me, install some security cameras, and please, please, take my dad off night duty tonight," Alicia pleaded.

Sharon sighed. "I'll agree to this: Your dad will be on night duty until midnight, then someone else will take his place." Seeing that Alicia was about to object, Sharon raised her hand. "That's the best deal you're going to get." Against Alicia's protests, she and her mother were escorted out of Sharon's office.

Sophia Zhong

Fortunately, Alicia's father survived the night. There was no invasion while he was on duty. However, the next morning the family was woken by a call from Sharon. "The zoo got raided again last night after your shift," she told Alicia's dad. "Can you and your family come over?" Alicia and her parents were anxious to see the footage from the new security cameras, so they got ready as fast as they could and drove to the zoo to meet with Sharon.

When the whole family was seated in her office, Sharon played the camera footage. It showed a young black-haired woman dressed in Greek armor riding a horse through the opening in the broken fence. More female warriors poured out of the woods behind her. They broke into some enclosures, lassoed the animals, and rode away with them, but not before taking night watchman Xavier Rackaley too. He had relieved Alicia's father of night watch at midnight.

Suddenly, Alicia had an idea. The Amazons wouldn't hurt an innocent child, especially a girl…would they? She had to talk to the queen of the Amazons alone. Alicia pitched the idea, but her parents weren't too enthusiastic about it. They finally agreed to let her try it once, but only because there was a chance many lives could be saved. Alicia was very excited and nervous because the stakes were so high.

That night, Alicia sat on a bench by the zoo's fence, while her parents waited outside the zoo. She heard hoofbeats thundering toward the hole in the fence. Alicia jumped up in time to see a dark figure racing through.

It was a beautiful young woman on a

majestic black horse. More warriors poured in behind her.

Alicia took a deep breath and called, "Queen Sapanaya!" The figure in the lead slowed and then stopped her horse. The young woman dismounted smoothly and stepped into a patch of moonlight.

"That would be me," she said in a melodious voice. "Who might you be?"

"My name is Alicia Vanschink. I'm here to speak to you." She sat down on the bench, and so did the queen. "Do you have a family?" Alicia asked. The question seemed to take the queen by surprise.

"I – yes, I do."

"So you know what love is like." The queen nodded. "Queen Sapanaya, the people you and your tribe have killed so far all have families. Right now, they're mourning their lost husbands, or fathers, or sons, or brothers. My dad was on night watch before you came last night. Would you have killed him?" Alicia asked.

"If we knew he was there, we would have taken him with us, but the tradition of the Amazons says that we must first hear him out," Queen Sapanaya replied. "The two night watchmen we have taken are not dead. We haven't had time to hold a trial, and we cannot consider whether to kill them or not until we do."

Alicia felt better. "That's good news! Still, do you realize what you're doing? You're hurting us all. If you had taken my father, you would have cut my whole family so deeply we could never heal. Even though you didn't take him, you did take Xavier Rackaley. If you continue to raid the zoo, it will close forever.

What will happen to all those people who rely on their jobs at the zoo to put food on the table?" Alicia asked. "Queen Sapanaya, you must stop. Please. Maybe you can speak with the owner of the zoo, Bill Myor, and we can arrange something, a deal. At least give it a chance."

Queen Sapanaya sat in silence. At last she spoke. "I am surprised to hear all this coming from such a young girl. Your courage and concern for others has led me to consider that perhaps not all unbelievers are bad and wish to destroy nature. I am willing to try to talk things out with the zoo owner. When will we meet?"

Alicia was overjoyed. "Can you come back here tomorrow at noon without any warriors? And can you bring Ronald Donacker and Xavier Rackaley with you?"

"I can do that," the queen said.

"One other thing," Alicia said. "If you hear this," - she whistled - "it means go back to the forest. The owner of the zoo might not want to meet with you."

"Understood. But the owner must be made aware that if he doesn't meet with me, we will keep raiding the zoo and taking whoever gets in our way," the queen warned. "Even if we do meet, that doesn't mean I'll decide to stop raiding the zoo," she added hastily as she mounted her horse.

"I know," Alicia sighed. "I'll do my best. See you tomorrow!" she called. The queen nodded at her from atop the horse, blew her gold horn, and galloped away with her warriors. Alicia went back to the RV with her parents and slept fitfully.

The next day, Alicia and her parents met

with the owner of the zoo, Bill Myor. Alicia told him about the agreement she and the queen had made: For them to meet and work things out. He decided to meet with Queen Sapanaya if Alicia would go with him. Her parents agreed to wait for her outside the zoo.

When they were ready, Alicia quickly led Bill to the place where she had talked to the queen.

"Come on! She's waiting!" Alicia called to Bill over her shoulder as she approached the queen.

Queen Sapanaya stood in front of them by the bench. Ronald Donacker and Xavier Rackaley were standing a few yards away. Their hands were bound behind their backs and they were blindfolded, but they were alive. The meeting began.

After Alicia introduced Bill Myor and

Queen Sapanaya, she proposed the deal she had thought up: With every litter of two or more animal babies, the zoo could keep one baby and the rest the Amazons would set free. One Amazon warrior would keep an eye on the zoo and tell the queen if any babies were due. Also, the two night watchmen would be released, and the Amazons wouldn't take any more zoo employees or their families. Queen Sapanaya and Bill both agreed to the deal, and it was sealed.

The queen cut the two night watchmen's bonds and freed them. Soon after, all of them departed except for Alicia.

As soon as she was alone, Alicia sank down onto the bench. She was shocked that she had actually done what no one had ever done before. She was only ten years old, and she had negotiated a treaty between an owner

of a zoo and the Queen of the Amazons. In doing so, she had saved the lives of countless people, including her father.

When Alicia had recovered, she joined her parents and they all went off to celebrate… and get ice cream.

Afterward, Alicia established a long friendship with Queen Sapanaya, and the ghost of Edgar Westcock never bothered her or the museum again.

THE END

Author's Note

In writing this book, I tried to include some realistic and factual points.

The Amazon Rainforest does exist. The Amazon Museum does not. Neither does Haunted Woods National Park.

Anacondas, black panthers, crocodiles, giant anteaters, jaguars, monkeys, ocelots, pink river dolphins, piranhas, poison dart frogs, scarlet macaws, sloths, tapirs, and toucans all live either in the Amazon Rainforest or Amazon River.

The aphandra is a real tree in the Amazon, but it lives in more than one area in the rainforest.

All the characters in this book are from my imagination.

As for the Amazons, no one knows whether the rainforest was named for them.

I, personally, got the idea from Greek mythology.

Edgar mentions Ares, the Greek god of war, and Artemis, the Greek goddess of the hunt, maidens, moon, and wild animals. They are the patron gods of the Amazons.

The golden belt Queen Sapanaya wears is a special belt that was passed down from the first Amazon queen. Heracles, better known by his Roman name, Hercules, had to retrieve it as one of his labors.

However, I made up the part about the Amazons living as long as they wished.

Acknowledgements

I would like to thank writer M.A. Moone for editing and commenting on this book. I would also like to thank Cora Quinn (GG) for arranging for me to read this book to my first audience. Thank you, Mom and Dad, Fay and Ray Zhong, for supporting me in every way possible. Thank you, Aunt DeAnne, for editing this book countless times. Lastly, thank you, Uncle Brad, for doing the beautiful illustrations.

- Sophia Zhong

Background

In June of 2016, my godparents took me and my family to the Oregon Coast. While there, we visited many shops and bookstores. Most of them had ghost stories.

Uncle Brad challenged me to write a ghost story before the vacation was over – basically two weeks. I was really excited, and I thought of it everywhere: at Crabby's Bakery, when we went sightseeing and kayaking, and especially in bookstores.

Well, I finished before the two weeks were up. When we got home, the real work started. Editing a book that's going to be published is no piece of cake.

- Sophia Zhong

About The Author

Sophia Zhong lives in California with her parents. She goes to Foothill Country Day School in Claremont, where she is an excellent student.

Sophia absolutely loves to read (and that's an understatement). She also plays the piano, sings, dances, takes speech and debate, and writes.

She is fascinated by all mythology, although her favorite is Greek mythology.

Sophia wrote this book when she was ten years old. She wrote and illustrated her first book, The Boss Bat, when she was four. She has been writing ever since.

In 2018, she entered Mrs. Nelson's Young Writers Contest, which encompasses all of Southern California, with her story entitled, The True Story Behind Pearl Harbor. She won first place.

The illustrator is her godfather, whom she calls Uncle Brad.

To learn more about Sophia or to read more of her written work, visit her web site at www.sophiazhong.com or get in contact with her at sophia@goddaughtersink.com.

About The Illustrator

Brad Appleby lives in Southern Nevada. He works in marketing and is a photographer, artist, troubleshooter and purveyor of endless great ideas. He and his wife DeAnne love traveling and often visit Sophia and her family and travel with them. You can contact him at brad@applebyarts.com or visit his website at www.applebyarts.com.

Look for Brad's logo hidden in each illustration in this book.

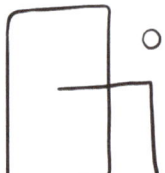